DATE DUE

DISCARD

GAYLORD   PRINTED IN U.S.A.

For brave mice everywhere

Library of Congress Cataloging-in-Publication Data

Morgan, Michaela.
Brave, Brave Mouse / by Michaela Morgan; illustrated by Michelle Cartlidge.
p. cm.
Summary: After showing courage by trying many new things, Little Mouse becomes Brave Mouse
when he realizes that it is sometimes good to say no to things he is not ready to try.
ISBN 0-8075-0869-1 (hardcover)
[1. Courage–Fiction. 2. Mice–Fiction.] I. Cartlidge, Michelle, ill. II. Title.
PZ7.M8255Br 2004   [E]–dc22   2003023874

Originally published in the United Kingdom in 2004 by Frances Lincoln Ltd.

Text copyright © 2004 by Michaela Morgan.
Illustrations copyright © 2004 by Michelle Cartlidge.
Published in 2004 by Albert Whitman & Company,
6340 Oakton Street, Morton Grove, Illinois 60053-2723.
Published simultaneously in Canada by Fitzhenry & Whiteside, Markham, Ontario.
Printed in Singapore.
10 9 8 7 6 5 4 3 2 1

For more information about Albert Whitman & Company,
please visit our web site at www.albertwhitman.com.

Brave, Brave Mouse

by Michaela Morgan
illustrated by Michelle Cartlidge

ALBERT WHITMAN & COMPANY, MORTON GROVE, ILLINOIS

Little Mouse was scared of all sorts of things.

Dark shadows scared him.

Bright lights scared him.

Loud noises scared him.

And silence scared him, too.

One day Mom and Dad said, "We're
going out for a while. The babysitter will look
after you until we get back."

Little Mouse did not like this one bit. His ears began to droop.

His whiskers began to twitch.

A big tear started to run down his nose.

Then a little voice inside him said,

They'll be back soon. Wait and see.
You're a brave mouse—as brave as brave can be!

And Little Mouse took a deep breath
and waved bye-bye.

And later, they DID come back, and they hugged
him and they loved him and they stroked his little ears.

"What a big brave mouse you are!" said Mom.

The first time Little Mouse went to the swimming pool, he didn't like it one bit.

He stood and he shivered.

His ears drooped.

His whiskers quivered.

The water looked cold and deep.
It smelled funny and everything was so LOUD.

Then a little voice inside him said,

Perk up your whiskers. Dip in a toe.
You're a brave, brave mouse, so give it a go!

Little Mouse did give it a go. And he loved it!

He splished

and he **splashed**

and he **sploshed**

until it was time
to go home.

Little Mouse did all sorts of brave things.

Go on. Try a bit. Take a little bite.
You're a brave, brave mouse.
It might taste all right!

You're a brave, brave mouse—open wide.
Let the dentist peek inside.

It's only a shadow in the night.
If you reach out, you can switch on the light.

One day, Little Mouse went to the playground.
There were swings, a big shiny slide,
a wibbly-wobbly bridge, and a
bouncing duck. The children shouted
to Little Mouse...

"Swing high
like me!"

"Slide fast
like me!"

But Little Mouse didn't really want to climb high or slide fast that day.

Then the little voice inside him said,

Are you going to give it a go?
You ARE a brave, brave mouse,
you know.

And Brave Mouse said...

"No!"

Brave Mouse stood up tall and bravely,
very bravely, made up his own mind.

"It's the bouncing duck for me!" he said.

Brave Mouse played happily and as he played,
he sang a little song…

Sometimes I do.
Sometimes I don't.
Sometimes I try new things.
Sometimes I won't.
I can be brave, the bravest of all.
I can brush my whiskers and stand up tall.
I can speak up, I can squeak up.
So look at me.
I am Brave Mouse.
Brave, Brave Mouse,
that's me!